Cesar

TAKES A BREAK

written by
SUSAN COLLINS THOMS

illustrated by
ROGÉ

STERLING

New York / London

WEDNESDAY

My name is Cesar, and I am one lucky green iguana.
I live in Ms. Lee's second-grade classroom at
Pinebrook Elementary School. I have 25 best friends.
They feed me mangoes. They spritz me with water.
They tell me their secrets.

Sometimes, they shower me with gifts. Today, thanks
to David's karate kick, I got my own journal and pen.
Just like my friends, I can write my life story.
It will be sensational.

Pet Shop

It's hard to believe that just three months ago, I was in Pets-A-Plenty, trying to choose the perfect person to adopt me. I was very choosy. Then, Ms. Lee brought me to Pinebrook Elementary for a trial visit.

One look, and I knew I was home.

Now, I wonder how this class
ever managed without me.

THURSDAY

As usual, I kept the class running smoothly all day.
Helped Luanne do the weather report. Reminded
Ramon of the computer password. (Hint: It's my name!)
Announced lunchtime by flicking my tongue.
And kept watch during storytime. Swish! A swing
of my tail told Ms. Lee to turn the page.
At 3:15, I bobbed my head.
"Class dismissed!" Ms. Lee said.

FRIDAY

Terrible news!

Today, Ms. Lee announced something awful: Spring Break. Everyone is leaving for a week. Only Mr. Will, the custodian, is staying to take care of me.

I slumped in my cage, shocked. My friends just cheered and ran out the door.

"See ya next week, Cesar!" was all they said.

How can they be happy?

I am a puddle of sadness.

SATURDAY

Too lonesome to eat.
Too bored to write.

SUNDAY

~~Too sad~~ ... ~~Too blue~~ ... ~~Too pitiful~~ ...
Enough moping!
Tomorrow, I'm taking a break, just like my friends.
And I know where I want to go.
Pinebrook Elementary, here I come!

MONDAY

Packed up my journal, grabbed some grapes for the road, and pushed open the classroom door. I scampered to the top of the lockers and scanned the hall. It was big and dark. But I was brave. Very brave.

I crept along until I saw the principal's office. And that's when I got a brilliant idea.
Click, Click. Next year's Spring Break was cancelled.
Click. Mr. Will got a nice raise.
Click. Click. Lunch menus were new and improved.
The kids will <u>love</u> spinach soufflé five times a week!
I took a spin in the swivel chair. Ha! I love being in charge.

Dizzy but hungry, I followed my flicking tongue to the cafeteria.

Salad heaven!

I was feasting on strawberries and spinach when I heard a squeaky voice.

"And they call _me_ a pig."

It was another class pet, a guinea pig named Sassy. Leapin' lettuce, that pig sure fixed a fancy feast.

After lunch, Sassy and I
had a blast! Went bowling.
Crash! I love strikes.

Filled up the sink
and went for a swim.
Sassy couldn't believe
how long I could hold
my breath.

Then we got
toasty warm under the
French-fry heat lamps.

Exhausted, we curled up for the night in the Lost and Found.

"Do you think the kids from Ms. Lee's room miss me?" I asked.

"Just as much as you miss them," Sassy said. And she fell asleep.

I lay awake and wondered about my friends. Were they having fun? Were they making new friends?

And did their new friends snore as loud as Sassy?

TUESDAY

Sassy told me to return to my classroom this morning.
"Stay until Mr. Will feeds you, so he won't start
looking for you," she said.

After he left, I visited Sassy's room. It's the best!

I tail-painted. She paw-painted.

We built pyramids.

We magnified ourselves. Oo-wee, I look even better
up close.

I asked Sassy if she knew any other class pets.

"Come to the gym tomorrow," she said.

WEDNESDAY

There was a class pet basketball tournament today!
Hoo boy, was I good. Made only one shot, but it won
the game. I celebrated by doing the Iguana Shuffle.
"Cesar, you belong on a stage," Sassy said.
That Sassy knows a star when she sees one!

THURSDAY

Went to the stage this morning and picked out a
costume just my style. Hail Cesar!
Sassy turned on the green lights, and I strutted out.
"To blend or not to blend, that is the question."
The audience went wild.
My tail quivered with joy.

Sassy turned on a pink light.
"Change color," she said.
I refused.
"Green is the only color for me."
Everyone booed.
I snapped my tail at them and left.

Backstage, I bumped into a turtle.

"Out of my way, slowpoke," I said. "Who are you, anyway?"

"Name's Peace, and I'm off to see the world." The turtle smiled. "You're looking pretty low, son. Why don't you go to the music room? That always cheers me up."

In the music room, I sat at the piano and played the blues.

POOR, POOR CESAR,

SO SAD, SO SAD.

MISS MY REAL FRIENDS

SO BAD, SO BAD.

I felt much better.

Sassy and the other pets showed up.
We all apologized. And then we danced:

THE GOLDFISH FLOP.

THE GUINEA PIG HUSTLE.

AND THE IGUANA SHUFFLE.

My new friends are real friends, after all.

FRIDAY

Today we played hockey in the teacher's lounge until we lost the puck.

"Let's use Peace for a puck," said a rabbit.

"Not Peace!" I said. "He's off to see the world."

"He does that every Spring Break," Sassy said. "He never makes it past the front door."

"Still," I said, "we should give Peace a chance."

SATURDAY

We met in the library today. That place has a million books!

I read <u>Reptiles Rule</u>, and Sassy read <u>Mighty Mammals</u>. Then we switched, and I learned a thing or two about fur.

There was a huge ball in a fancy stand. I suggested we use it to play soccer.

"That's no ball," Sassy said. "It's the world. See the oceans? See the land?"

I got another brilliant idea.

Lickety split, I was in the halls, hunting for Peace.
"Climb aboard," I said. "There's something
you gotta see."

Then, I brought Peace to the world.
I felt pretty good about that.
I think Peace was happy, too.

SUNDAY

Today, I met a wild mouse named Nibbles. She used to be a class pet, but she escaped last Spring Break. Now, she has a cozy nest in the furnace room with a door that leads right to the playground.

That got me thinking: Should I stay on Spring Break forever, too?

The things I would do!

Surf in Hawaii. Climb Mount Everest. Maybe I would become the first iguana to fly to the moon.

Sassy said, "That's just plain silly. When vacation is over, class pets go home. End of story."

Peace said, "Follow your heart. Go to Ms. Lee's room. Think it over there."

I walked around the classroom and soaked up the sights and smells of home. It felt good to be there. Really good.

I imagined my friends coming to school tomorrow and finding my empty cage. They would be 25 puddles of sadness.

And, boy, would they be lost! Who would listen to their secrets? Help them with schoolwork? Tell them when it was lunchtime?

I told Sassy and Peace
my mind was made up.

MONDAY

I'm back and I'm glad!

I'm happy to see my friends, and they are so happy to see me.

And this class needs me now more than ever. They are studying reptiles! How could they do that without me?

I'm also learning important stuff. The walls are covered with my friends' pictures from Spring Break. I'm getting ideas. Lots of ideas. Lots of good, gotta-do-it, fun vacation ideas.

Wee-hee, I can't wait until the next vacation!

I sure hope we get a summer break.

A FEW FASCINATING FACTS
ABOUT GREEN IGUANAS by Cesar

- Iguanas hatch from eggs and start out small, but we can grow to be six feet long. I might be longer than you someday!

- It's great to be green! Our color helps us blend in with a leafy background. But we don't change our color to match our surroundings.

- It's no problem getting iguanas to eat our fruits and veggies. That's about all we eat!

- Like other reptiles, we are cold-blooded, which means we don't produce our own body heat. To get warm, we like to bask in the sun (or under a French-fry warming light if there's one handy).

- In the wild, green iguanas live high in the trees in tropical rain forests. (Ms. Lee's room is wild enough for me.) When we get scared, we climb to a high place until we feel safe again.

- We have: Sharp claws that are great for climbing. A tongue that we use to taste the air and nearby objects. A long tail that we can snap at predators to scare them away. If something grabs it, the tail breaks off, but then it grows back. (Ouch! I hope I never lose my tail.)

  - We are great divers and swimmers. We can hold our breath under water for almost half an hour! (Guess I should have told Sassy that, so she wouldn't worry.)

  - The flap of skin under an iguana's chin is called a dewlap. We puff it up to make ourselves look bigger. It helps scare off predators. Take that, scaredy-cat!

  - An iguana likes to bob its head. It's our way of saying "I'm in charge here." And sometimes we do it to scare away enemies.

- Iguanas are diurnal (like you). That means we sleep at night and play during the day. No nighttime prowling for me— I need my beauty sleep.

For Mom and Dad, my first and favorite storytellers.
And for David, who found Cesar. —S. C. T.

For Laïla and Aidan, who begin to discover the world. —Rogé

STERLING and the distinctive Sterling logo are registered trademarks of Sterling Publishing Co., Inc.

Library of Congress Cataloging-in-Publication Data

Thoms, Susan Collins.
Cesar takes a break / Susan Collins Thoms ; illustrated by Rogé.
p. cm.
Summary: While the children of Pinebrook Elementary School are on vacation, Cesar, the classroom iguana, decides to take his own spring break, during which he discovers the other school pets exploring all the wonders the school has to offer, from the music room to the cafeteria. Includes facts about green iguanas.
ISBN-13: 978-1-4027-3653-7
ISBN-10: 1-4027-3653-3
[1. Green iguana—Fiction. 2. Green iguanas as pets—Fiction. 3. Iguanas—Fiction. 4. Iguanas as pets—Fiction. 5. Schools—Fiction. 6. Animals—Fiction.] I. Rogé, 1972- ill. II. Title.
PZ7.T37372Ce 2008
[Fic]—dc22   2007036273

1 2 3 4 5 6 7 8 9 10

Published by Sterling Publishing Co., Inc.
387 Park Avenue South, New York, NY 10016
Text © 2008 by Susan Collins Thoms
Illustrations © 2008 by Rogé
The artwork was prepared using acrylic paints.
Distributed in Canada by Sterling Publishing
c/o Canadian Manda Group, 165 Dufferin Street
Toronto, Ontario, Canada M6K 3H6
Distributed in the United Kingdom by GMC Distribution Services
Castle Place, 166 High Street, Lewes, East Sussex, England BN7 1XU
Distributed in Australia by Capricorn Link (Australia) Pty. Ltd.
P.O. Box 704, Windsor, NSW 2756, Australia

Sterling   ISBN-13: 978-1-4027-3653-7
           ISBN-10: 1-4027-3653-3

For information about custom editions, special sales, premium and corporate purchases, please contact Sterling Special Sales Department at 800-805-5489 or specialsales@sterlingpublishing.com.

Designed by Scott Piehl